D0131106

Dr. Blackfoot's Carnival Extraordinaire

Written & Illustrated by

Ron Chatalbash

David R. Godine - Publisher - Boston

First published in 1982 by

David R. Godine, Publisher, Inc.
306 Dartmouth Street
Boston, Massachusetts 02116

Library of Congress Cataloging in Publication Data

Chatalbash, Ron, 1959–
   Dr. Blackfoot's carnival extraordinaire.

   Summary: Tim is so discouraged and bored by life
at home and school that he seizes a chance to join a
circus, not knowing what really awaits him.
   [1. Circus – Fiction]   I. Title.
PZ7.C3879Dr.   [Fic]   81-85126
ISBN 0-87923-426-1   AACR2

First edition

Printed in the United States of America

For David Lord Porter

With special thanks to Diane S. Boyce and Garrick Evans

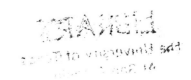

Tim longed to join the circus. He thought about nothing else by day and dreamt about nothing else at night. To Tim, the circus stood for everything fun in this world. Everything else — parents nagging him to clean his room and teachers bugging him to do his homework — was just plain boring. And even though no circus had ever come to his town, he still waited and wished, for he was certain one would come some day. When asked why, he'd say, 'Well, it just *has* to.'

And late one night, while Tim was lying awake dreaming and everyone else was sleeping, something very much like a circus *did* come. On the road, right below Tim's window, a trail of wagons moved slowly by. They were far more marvelous than anything he had seen in his picture books. And as he watched the last wagon roll past, he could make out gold lettering that said: *Dr. Blackfoot's Carnival Extraordinaire. Side Shows a Specialty.*

'Carnival Extraordinaire,' thought Tim. 'Not quite a circus, but close enough.'

He whispered goodbye to his cowardly dog Erasmutt and quietly climbed out of the window, down the trellis, and out onto the street.

The Carnival had left a wake of white handbills. Picking one up, Tim read:

Come see the Carnival
Extraordinaire.
Just follow the trail,
and you'll be there.

He stuffed the invitation in his pocket and ran down the street, following the paper trail to the edge of town.

Rounding a corner, Tim stopped in surprise. Before him was the Carnival. Everything was completely set up and ready for business. But there was no one in sight, and the only sounds to be heard were the tent flaps rustling in the breeze and the soft hum of the electric lights.

Suddenly Tim heard something move behind him. Whirling around to see who it was, he slipped on a handbill and landed next to his very nervous dog. 'I see you've decided to come along after all, Erasmutt,' said Tim, picking himself up. Then in a much softer tone he said, 'But since you're here, I guess there's no sense in making you go back home.' And the two gingerly took their first steps onto the deserted Carnival grounds.

All at once, a smiling, sly-looking clown popped out from a ticket booth.

'Hi ya, kid. He's in there waiting for you,' he said, pointing at a wagon.

Confused by this sudden appearance, Tim could only ask, 'Who?'

'Why, the good Dr. Blackfoot. The Ringmaster to you.' The clown smiled broadly, showing a large gold tooth. 'Go ahead. Walk right in. I'll be seeing you around.'

'Why should anyone be waiting for me?' Tim asked Erasmutt, since the clown was now nowhere to be seen. Erasmutt just cowered at his heels and reluctantly followed him up the creaky steps to the wagon door. A voice called from inside, 'Come in, friend.'

Tim walked into a room dimly lit by a glass sphere that seemed to hang in the air all by itself. The Ringmaster was seated in an ornately carved chair. 'So you want to join our little Carnival?' he asked. Tim nodded hesitantly, as Erasmutt crept into a corner, hoping not to be noticed. The Ringmaster snapped his fingers, and the floating sphere glowed, revealing a room cluttered with circus posters and books.

'After all, we're here because you wished us to be. Now that you've seen us, I'm sure you'll decide to leave your rather boring life. Of course, you realize that once you join us, you will belong to us. It's one or the other, Tim.' The Ringmaster smiled, and behind him Tim heard the door shut quietly.

'I think you'll be very happy here, Tim,' said the Ring-master, picking up a large magician's wand and a top hat. 'We never do *anything* ordinary or dull. It's not an easy life, but one thing I can promise, you won't be bored. But now let me introduce you to some of my friends — they've so looked forward to meeting you.' With that, the orb glowed even more brightly, lighting up the rest of the room. Tim realized that standing quite close to him were some of the strangest, scariest people he had ever seen: a strong man with moving tattoos, a two-headed man, a living skeleton, and a sharp-toothed midget, who was already eyeing Erasmutt greedily.

'Don't be alarmed, my boy. They're just curious to see what kind of boy chooses to join the circus. They had no choice, you see. It may take a while, but I'm sure you'll all get used to each other. Until then, I'd suggest you watch your step.'

Tim was getting very, very worried. He wasn't at all sure that he really wanted to be in the Carnival *forever*. This wonderful dream was rapidly becoming a nightmare. Even if his wishing *had* brought the Carnival here, he knew now it wasn't the answer to his problems. Quite suddenly, he wanted to be back home in his bed. He turned to run.

But as he moved toward the door, the Ringmaster rose from his chair and the others loomed closer, almost pinning Tim to the wall. Stabbing his cane at Tim, the Ringmaster said, 'It's not going to be that easy. If we didn't have a choice, why should you?' The orb glowed brighter and brighter.

Now Tim was really frightened. What on earth could he do? Helplessly, he looked at Erasmutt, and his expression must have lighted something in that cowardly dog's heart, for Erasmutt did something brave for the first time in his life. Leaping from his corner, he grabbed the midget's leg in his jaws, and the astonished midget let out such a shriek that everybody turned to see what was happening.

This was Tim's chance. Ducking under the Ringmaster's arm, he grabbed the wand from his outstretched hand. And then he did the only thing he thought might help: with a mighty swing, he smashed the orb.

Tim awoke to find himself in the middle of an open field. The Carnival had disappeared, and Tim couldn't even be sure that it had ever been there. Hugging Erasmutt, Tim said, 'You're not such a coward after all, Erasmutt. I guess I've taken a lot of things for granted lately. And it was pretty dumb of me to think that joining the circus would solve anything. I'm lucky I don't have to live the life those people lead. It all seems like a very bad dream. Let's go home.'

Back in his room, as he was getting ready for bed, Tim noticed something white flutter from his pocket to the floor. It looked a great deal like the handbill he had thoughtlessly stuffed into his pocket earlier that night. Had the Carnival been real after all? But as he reached to pick it up, a sudden breeze swept the paper over the floor and out the window. Staring after it, Tim wondered if he had seen it in the first place.

Much later, when Tim and Erasmutt were safely asleep, a sly-looking old bum picked up a crumpled piece of paper and smiled. His gold tooth gleamed softly in the first light of dawn.

DR. BLACKFOOT'S
CARNIVAL EXTRAORDINAIRE

has been set in a film version of Trump Mediæval,
a typeface designed by Professor Georg Trump in the
mid-1950s and cast by the C. E. Weber Typefoundry
of Stuttgart, West Germany. The roman letter forms
of Trump Mediæval are based on classical prototypes,
but have been interpreted by Professor Trump in a
distinctly modern style. The italic letter forms are
more of a sloped roman than a true italic in design,
a characteristic shared by many contemporary type-
faces. The result is a modern and distinguished type,
notable both for its legibility and its versatility.

The text was composed by Roy McCoy, Cambridge,
Massachusetts, printed in duotone by Eastern Press,
New Haven, Connecticut, and bound by Robert Burlen
& Son, Inc., Hingham, Massachusetts. The paper
is Warren's Lustro, an entirely acid-free sheet.